Goldilocks

and the

THREE POLAR BEARS

~ by Ross Murray ~

First edition April 2016

Art direction by Christopher Herndon
Cover by Ross Murray
Book layout by Christopher Herndon
_____

Library of Congress Cataloging-in-Publication Data

Murray, Ross, author, illustrator.
 Goldilocks and the Three Polar Bears / by Ross Murray. -- First edition.
    pages cm
 Audience: Age 5-10
 Audience: K to grade 4

First hardcover edition ISBN: 9781940052236

Portland, OR
www.craigmorecreations.com

Printed in Canada

For Ella

My father and I have just moved to a small town on the North Slope of Alaska. Dad is a helicopter pilot and he has got a job flying workers out to a new oil rig in the sea.

The first time I'm allowed to fly out to sea with Dad is very exciting.
The oil rig has big bright yellow pontoons. I tell Dad we should call it 'Goldilocks.'

On the way home I spot three bears down on the ice.
Dad says they're probably off to steal some porridge from Goldilocks and I laugh.
He knows how much I love polar bears so flies down to take a closer look.

I'm so thrilled to see real, live polar bears.
I give them a big wave out the window as we fly away home.

It's dinner time when we get back.
I ask Dad what the polar bears will be eating for dinner.
"Probably a delicious seal or maybe some seabirds," he tells me.

I ask him if we can see the bears right up close next time.
"When people and nature mix too closely, you never know what will happen," Dad says.
"Some things are best left alone. And we certainly wouldn't want them
to mistake you for their next meal!"

That night, I have a wonderful dream.

Dad and I make some more trips out over the ice.
I tell my new friends at school all about meeting the three bears.

Not long after that, something terrible happens in the night.

In the morning we fly out to the rig.
There has been a huge oil spill.

Over the side of the rig I watch sea birds dive for fish
and come up covered in thick black oil.

I see the polar bears on the way home and feel worried.

Over the next few days, the oil on the water is set on fire to try to stop it spreading.
I ask Dad to check on the bears on his way out to the rig.

The oil keeps burning for two weeks.
Then chemicals are poured into the sea to help break up the oil that is left.

The oilmen say they are cleaning up the ocean
but Dad tells me it will take many, many years for the sea and ice to get better.
The oil rig is going to be shut down so we will have to move away again.

I go out to the oil rig in the helicopter one last time.
I search and search for the three bears but I cannot find them.

I think about my dream and hope it has come true.

Ross is a New Zealand-based artist who loves telling stories. An acclaimed illustrator and comics creator, he's also passionate about nature and the environment. In 2011 he experienced firsthand the devastating effects of an oil spill on the beach outside his home at Mount Maunganui. This disaster combined with a desire for his two young children to grow up in a clean and healthy world inspired him to write this book.

A portion of the sales from each book goes to help support GREENPEACE